Ascension

Ebonye S. White

Copyright © 2019 Ebonye S. White

All rights reserved.

ISBN: 978-1-0773-0482-6

DEDICATION

This book is dedicated to my beautiful mother Verda T. White- Coates. Not for the content within, but for the simple fact that I still hear her beautiful confident soothing voice referring to me as her winner. If it were not for her introducing my sisters and I to everyone as her Winners I don't know where I would be or if I would have made it this far. I thank GOD for her. Thanks, Mom, for constantly watching over me and speaking to me when direction is needed. Thanks for being my angel. Thanks for pushing me. Thanks for covering me even in Paradise. Continue to rest well beloved.

CONTENTS

	Acknowledgments	i
	A Letter to My Readers	viii
	Introduction	ix
1	Concept of "The Dream"	Pg 1
2	Relentless Love	Pg 11
3	The Reality of Running	Pg 22
4	Critical Moments	Pg 31
5	Evolve	Pg 39
6	Natural Order	Pg 48
7	Strength in Me	Pg 56

ACKNOWLEDGMENTS

GOD has placed some amazing people in my life. You all know who you are. The daily inspirational messages, videos, conversations, and professional pointers mean the WORLD to me. My dearest sweetheart, thank you for encouraging me to approach my goals and dreams even if it means tackling the smallest first and then working my way up. All that you have done has shaped me into the undefeatable ultra-determined professional that I am. To my phenomenal cousin David, you have been the best accountability partner that a woman could ask for. Thank you so much for the advice and for PUSHing (Pray Until Something Happens) for and with me to new heights. Your prayer, patience, and encouragement has blessed me in more ways than you can imagine. Kendra Nicholson; thank you for volunteering to read my book and giving feedback even while taking care of my beautiful GOD-son Syree.

Raelynn Lambert, your attention to detail and your quick call to action after my request for you to look over a chapter for me is more than greatly appreciated. Thanks for always picking up where we leave off and adding substance each time we connect. You have been more than a friend and former co-worker. You have been a true sister to me. Ms. Rhonda Baker, I thank you for thinking quick on your feet any and every time I came up with an idea or business venture. You were always ready to connect me with a reputable resource.

Dr. Lucas, I appreciate you for reviewing multiple sample covers to my book and encouraging me to move forward with this project before I made a final decision. To my sister Regina G. Groves, thank you for believing in everything that I do. You pushed me. You have been my second wind. Grandma, Delores White, we have had many conversations and you have watched me shed many tears over the years. You are one of the reasons why I am the confident, clean, and assertive woman I am today. Thank you so much for raising my sisters and I in the church. To my baby brother Jay, you have been the wind beneath my wings. I build for you. It's now your turn to carry the torch. I will continue to build a legacy and I am excited to see all that you achieve. I love you all immensely. Thank you all for supporting me.

A Letter to My readers

I pray this message finds you in the greatest health and spirits, for you to be covered in positivity, and to ultimately be enlightened after this piece. As you engage you will find yourself gaining insight into the seven areas of life. This book is purposely composed of only seven chapters as seven is the number of completion. I hope that you identify the tools you need to achieve your level of completion after reading Ascension in its entirety. From the first through the last page you will learn about balance as it pertains to relationships, finance, business, spiritual, physical health, family, and mental health. To ensure that you are being well informed of my intent from beginning through the conclusion; I have supplied you with intense detail of the thought process that went into this book. It is my full intention that this piece serves as a place of healing, enlightenment, and motivation.

Have you ever felt as though past and current decisions you're making are never right? Have you ever felt you were going to miss out on or destroy something if you made the wrong decision? Sometimes life forces you to make decisions. Given the fact that time waits for no one; no matter how much you delay- life will always force you to decide. Sometimes your decisions will throw a wrench in the plans of others and even your own. In other instances, you may miss out on things that are more exciting because you chose to follow your curiosity instead of the historical facts which would have helped you to make a better decision. Before you continue; ask yourself the following questions: Am I willing to stop talking about being successful and act? Am I willing to continue to wish I can achieve financial freedom, or will I do something about it? Am I willing to stop watching others win in front of me and become a winner myself? Am I prepared to simply act so that I can obtain that million-dollar reaction from clients, customers, friends, family, followers, fans, and lovers?

If so, reeeeeeaders take your marrrrrrks, seeeeeet, LET's GO! Come with me as I define resilience and completion through the lens of our main character Autumn using business as a driving force and tool.

Introduction

Mind filled with a million thoughts; I begin to settle into my creative self and write this book. No special thanks to anyone in particular; just those of you that decided to use, abuse, misuse, and rob me of my thoughts, time, and patience. Most importantly to the one that I entrusted my heart, mind, intellectual property, and finances to; you're no better than the rest. Salute!

While I'm no self-proclaimed relationship expert, I am an expert in my life, past mistakes, past victories, and an individual willing to help steer others away from the pitfalls that I've made so that you can be the best you. Not to mention; I am a licensed social worker who has helped many families, children, and adults work through plenty of personal issues, mental health difficulties, and necessary behavior adjustments if that counts for anything. **Warm Smile***

CHAPTER 1: Concept of "THE DREAM"
"The only tired I was; was tired of giving in." ~Rosa Parks

No pictures of unique experiences. Just memories. Extremely early mornings and even later nights; Autumn was plagued by anxiety. Thoughts of "possibility" that she had not tapped into resulted in disrupted sleep. No matter how soft or hard the mattress is or was; when her finances or livelihood were in jeopardy no mattress or lover stood a chance. Concerns of possibly not living up to her very own expectations blew her eyelids wide open as if someone were setting off fireworks of disturbances in her head. Riddled with migraines attributed to the fast clips that speed through her mind as if they were on the Autobahn in Germany exceeding 225 miles per hour. Even as Autumn slept; certain conversations jumped out at her as if they have gone one thousand miles per hour off Mt. Everest! Uncertainty and self- doubt lead Autumn to the face of anxiety and insecurity. Fear of failure kept her mind filled with thoughts of whether her honesty would adversely interfere with her destiny.

Frustrations of being trapped in the rat race resulting in debt and professional bondage were her greatest fears. Autumn promised herself in her early twenties that she would rescue herself from the rat race. The personal promise that she made never allowed Autumn to give up. For someone else, this type of pressure could mean the end for sure. Fear of failure while pregnant with possibility; Autumn aspired to make history, but how? She acknowledges and rewards her inner curiosities for being optimistic enough to continue thriving through the midst of all obstacles. Conversely, she still thought of ways in which she could make her mark.

For years the dream has been to love and live freely. Free of stress, regret, hurt, heartbreak, judgment, frustration, disappointment, fear, and confusion. Autumn was always afraid to spend money if she received assistance from a lover, a family member, or a friend. Fearful that they would frown upon her decision to treat herself. Fearful that she would disappoint them. Fearful that they would stop doing for her because she made a conscious decision to love and gift herself. Autumn decided that asking for help was not enough. To her it was not even worth it nor could it be an option. Autumn simply decided to suffer in silence until she could devise another plan to rescue herself. The dream consisted of experiences of pure peace of mind, body, spirit, finance, and genuine security in every respective area in life.

Being an optimistic individual sometimes allows you to come off as naive. On the flip side; you're taking risks that others frown upon in all effort and sacrifice to rise to the top. As lonely as people say things are at the top; when you're broke, heartbroken, and barely ever heard when spoken- it's even lonelier at the bottom. I bet you wonder how one can live fearlessly and be filled with fear at the same time? To live fearlessly could mean that you're not afraid to chase the dream, but to live in fear is to understand the reality of failure and the fact that it cannot be an option. Thus, it hinders you from taking steps forward that will increase your chances of growth. Those concerns reign true especially when you have no one else to turn to.

Living in a world where we feast off instant gratification and the fairytale of getting rich quick; many are willing to steal, kill, and destroy their way to success. Often; we're willing to trade up rather than sticking it out at the very bottom of the financial barrel. Very seldom do you find individuals willing to genuinely help without some sort of benefit. Bound by fear; it became nearly impossible for Autumn to realize that her throne was near. For instance, Autumn could not see "the one" who loved her the most because she was too busy chasing a love that "Mr. Right Now's" heart refused to host. In so many instances if Autumn had focused on saving, she would have already accomplished her goal of marriage, business grand openings, and financial freedom.

Had Autumn saved herself until marriage her superior decision-making abilities would not have been clouded in the past by lust. If she'd simply saved more money for her project than she spent on clothes and impressing ungrateful people; she would have already paid off all her debt. Day after day Autumn participated in the rat race that she dreaded. She grew weary and became leery of whether anything that she'd dreamed would ever come to fruition.

Go lives, system implementations, trauma care, youth advocacy, public speaking, team building, system development, and planning were her professional specialties. She couldn't seem to give herself enough patience, time, and effort to bring her visions to life. It was sad how effective she had been to everyone, but herself. Autumn kept telling herself how great she was at thinking on her feet and creating systems. She created systems and had so many grand ideas to implement for everyone else, but she continued to neglect herself in the process.

Out of all her experiences, Autumn realized that there was a theme that became extremely clear to her. That theme was "time." The reason being, she'd reach a point in which she needed to make time work for and with herself to fulfill the GOD given purpose placed on her life. She's been everyone else's greatest cheerleader and she now had no energy to even begin building herself. All she needed to do was implement her systems into her personal life and all that she'd set out to accomplish would begin to align itself exactly as they needed.

Once upon a time, Autumn knew beyond a reasonable doubt that she would be able to make her dreams along with a ton of other people's; a reality. Unfortunately, each year that she encountered a set back the light that once was so bright within her began to dime. Eventually, internally everything inside of her became too dark for her to see beyond her current reality. Autumn was filled with regret when she could have been filled with joy, financial freedom, and enjoying every moment of her life. Autumn learned the hard way that you must be very careful with love. She had mistaken lust for love, became too anxious for a partner, and was too eager for someone to elevate her in their life.

Unfortunately, she found herself with men who emotionally defeated her. As an individual, you must be very careful about whom you allow to occupy your time and love space. Understand that a broken individual can come into your life to disrupt, destroy, devastate, and even cause an avalanche of pain that you never would have willingly invited into your life. Autumn began to become a prisoner of her past. She sometimes thought to herself why am I not the type of female who puts money in front of love and relationships? Why have I always placed my emotions in front of opportunities that would elevate me? Perhaps the questions that she asked herself weren't socially acceptable, conservative enough to venture into modest circles, or could even seem to be self-explanatory, but she was concerned and needed to self-reflect and further evaluate her choices.

Autumn once read a short excerpt in which there was a reference to subway tunnels. It eluded to the fact that we as people tend to display very little fear when traveling into the dark tunnels on mass transportation. The reason being; we have factual reason to believe that there is another station, safety, and light beyond the darkness. This made her realize that sometimes it truly is necessary that we travel into darkness for us to get to our destination which in turn could bring us in contact with our next opportunity. Scenarios such as the previously mentioned dark tunnel and scriptures such as *Matthew 6:25-34* reminded her of GOD's promise to provide.

"25 "Therefore I tell you, do not worry about your life, what you will eat or drink; or about your body, what you will wear. Is not life more than food, and the body more than clothes? 26 Look at the birds of the air; they do not sow or reap or store away in barns, and yet your heavenly Father feeds them. Are you not much more valuable than they? 27 Can anyone of you by worrying can add a single hour to your life?
28 "And why do you worry about clothes? See how the flowers of the field grow. They do not labor or spin. 29 Yet I tell you that not even Solomon in all his splendor was dressed like one of these. 30 If that is how God clothes the grass of the field, which is here today and tomorrow is thrown into the fire, will he not much more clothe you—you of little faith? 31 So do not worry, saying, 'What shall we eat?' or 'What shall we drink?' or 'What shall we wear?' 32 For the pagans run after all these things, and your heavenly Father knows that you need them. 33 But seek first his kingdom and his righteousness, and all these things will be given to you as

well. 34 Therefore do not worry about tomorrow, for tomorrow will worry about itself. Each day has enough trouble of its own."

Autumn knew that she did not have to worry even in instances where she probably wanted to. Autumn continued to strive; doing what she felt was sacrificing in order to achieve her goals to make her dreams a reality. Day in and day out Autumn would pray and try to think of creative ways to execute her vision. The one challenge that she found herself confronted with the most was understanding and implementing- "How?" rather than asking herself repeatedly "why?" Relentlessly, she was trying to figure out a way to pay for everything instead of *coming up with ways in which things could begin to pay for themselves.* She would pray and ask GOD for direction, talk to her confidant, and even complete some much-needed reflection. Sadly, in her mind her efforts still turned up empty. It was as if her life was experiencing an overwhelming case of writer's block.

Nothing was seeming to come to her easily or naturally no matter how hard she worked or how much focus was involved. She thought to herself that relationship, nor business, nor cash flow yielded much return on her investment. What she failed to realize were her wins and blessings. She spent too much time focusing on things that did not go her way (relationships, expedited grand openings, and large amounts of fast cash) while missing all the benefits and blessings (long term assets such as her properties and investments) that were there stay. In her inexperienced mind, it was as if it all came to a screeching halt each time Autumn seemed to gain even the slightest bit of comfort, traction, and momentum. She wanted more liquid assets. She wanted out of the trial period of her blessings. She was ready to immediately reap the benefits. She was growing impatient. Her desire for financial freedom left her trying to figure out how to elevate herself to higher levels.

Sitting there with stress resting on her neck, shoulders, and back she still made every attempt to bounce back. Headaches for days wishing that she would come up with the next big thing that pays. Growing weary and even staring off into a daze; she hoped and prayed for better days. Autumn blamed herself for taking things for granted including those that she could not recall. She grew tired of trying to figure out people and things who felt they knew it all. She could not understand why her timing was so awful. It was as if she came into everything that she desired and even loved; at the wrong time. Day in and day out all she did was brainstorm, but she still felt as though her hard work resulted in mediocrity.

Feeling abandoned, she internalized everything. Autumn realized that the thing that she relied on to comfort her financially was detrimental to her progress and her health. That "thing" was her employer. Somehow, she manipulated herself into believing that there was financial security in having a "good-paying job." Reality set in the very first time that she was laid off due to a company restructuring, it set in once more when she was laid off due to scandal, and again when the company eliminated her position. She finally realized that companies use people the same way people use paper plates and prostitutes. You are good to purchase for temporary use, but once you've served your temporary purpose-they throw you out like rubbish. It is for that reason she reminds herself that she is not allowed to be distracted. She reminds herself and others that it is great to be personable, but never get personal (Great professional and business tip **wink wink**.)

Autumn realized that each time she let her guard down in any place of employment; discussing the highlights of her life, goals, self-employment plans, relationship satisfaction, or personal shortcomings; those things were used against her in both company and personal planning decisions. She found herself being forwarded an email sent to a new employer by a former supervisor that she adored and respected. The email was written to save her former supervisors tail in an instance of anger, vulnerability, an ultimate betrayal; after her former supervisor was dismissed from the new employer which acquired their old company. The email was retaliatory given Autumn was appointed to a position that her former supervisor thought she would be given.

The email incident helped Autumn to realize that when folks' backs are against the wall; loyalty breaks down quicker than cotton candy. Soon after she received advice from a very intelligent man that she will forever appreciate. That advice was "trust no one." In business, you must trust people to stay true to and take care of themselves no matter what. As long as you stand to win together you shall see great deeds blossom and loyalty reciprocated. Loyalty is tested when tough times arise, and one stands to lose everything. How many people do you know will be willing to risk it all to see you through?

Autumn once sat listening to the story of consistency that a young woman told; it resonated so well with her. Although she may not be able to note what the young woman said precisely; she does recall her speaking of the need for the caterpillar to remain consistent in eating for it to be able to elevate to the next phase. Initially, a butterfly starts as a caterpillar, then transitions into the cocoon, and ultimately blossoms into a beautiful butterfly. The butterfly analogy is relative to Autumn because she knows that she is capable of doing anything she desired as long as she stays consistent.

Many people around the world see the butterfly as a symbol of hope, change, endurance, life, and courage. Autumn was quickly able to relate to the butterfly's origins. She saw her process as a young child, young professional, and aspiring entrepreneurs in the same manner. She even respected the earlier struggles of the butterfly. Autumn was also reminded of her dear beloved Alya. She affectionately remembered her as a beautiful butterfly as she had a beautiful personality but was such a free spirit. She was born with so much potential, but tragically her life was cut too short. Alya was someone Autumn loved dearly and lost tragically to the streets.

Daily Autumn fantasized about her life. She envisioned herself evolving into an even better free spirit of the personality that she carried as a child. She visualized daily; moments in which she could board a private jet, take random flights for the day, have couple massages in flight, shop in and tour foreign countries, but be home by night. She pictured outings with a group of similarly successful friends, random couple excursions simply because she was so deserving. She constantly told herself that no matter how hard things had gotten she would not allow adversity to defeat or deter her. As she patiently waited for her time to spread her wings to fly and shine; she was continuously reminded of the many blessings sent by the divine.

With her life plagued with tragedy she was determined to make her mark in the world. Having lost both of her parents before completing college she prayed, pushed, and found alternative ways to motivate herself. She refused to allow setbacks to have victory. Autumn realized after she dropped her tears for both parents that there was no relationship in this world that she would fear. She promised herself not to become bitter, but instead, she would become much better. One challenge after another; determination became her strength. She learned the hard way that being naive was no way to survive. Education was everything. It would free her from so much. It took her the longest to realize what was meant by "education is paramount."

Whether or not you consider yourself to fit the mold or specific categories that society tends to group people in; the truth is; we all must face the "real," true, and total person we are as individuals at some point. In this chapter, we were introduced to Autumn. _The link between Profession, Finance, Love, and Mental Health_ were all previously depicted. Often, we do not recognize such links. Only recently has the medical field acknowledged that there is a clear link between mental and medical health. This is evident in the new trauma-informed care approach that most hospitals and clinics have adopted. It's clear that many may not acknowledge the fact that your financial positioning has a direct impact on your physical, mental, and emotional health. Children, teenagers, young adults alike are not being vastly taught that your first wages accepted when applying to jobs or starting career paths impact your future earnings. They are not being taught to establish multiple streams of income in impoverished communities early enough. Many are being conditioned to be direct reports and to help companies achieve their financial goals. Could you imagine the impact on various socio-economic groups if we were all exposed to the same knowledge? Think about the mental and physical impact that would benefit more individuals if financial coaches were available in schools, hospitals, and clinics.

Had Autumn learned about the links between proper and improper investments of time, money, and energy rather than having to experience it for herself; she would be in a better much healthier place. If only "she'd been given an opportunity and more exposure to personal finance, business development, and self-care; she would have been able to make more balanced and structured decisions"- she thought to herself. Autumn wish that she had someone reinforcing the need to save, invest early, open a business while she had no overhead. If only she'd heard someone tell her often to stay away from boys and take advantage of all progressive, and positive opportunities presented; the emotional decisions would not even be a question. She wished that she'd received similar advice from her father so that she would better understand relationships of every kind would test her. It was as if she inherently knew that she should never break or succumb to enticing words or challenges. She realized her potential, but not the core of how substantial it was. She realized that not only did she have a grace that covered her, but that she had so much within her. No matter the amount of neglect, trauma, or abandonment; Autumn realized that what is in her could never be taken away or duplicated. She realized that she is the only one that can execute the vision which lives deep within her.

Ascension

Checkmate Inventory

Life and love can be so beautiful yet disastrous and painful. So often we operate in a psychological fairytale that we often forget to take inventory of both ourselves and the relationships we engage in.

Do you feel energetic or drained in your mates' presence?

1. _____

Are you relaxed or stressed in your relationship?

2. _____

Do you feel loved, liked, tolerated, appreciated, or unappreciated?

3. _____

Do you feel you are in a toxic or healthy relationship?

4. _____

Do you feel motivated or are you lacking motivation in your relationship?

5. _____

Do you feel your time has been wasted or properly invested in your relationship?

6. _____

Do you feel your relationship is built on trust or fear?

7. _____

Chapter 2: Relentless Love

"6 Do not be anxious about anything, but in every situation, by prayer and petition, with thanksgiving, present your requests to God. 7 And the peace of God, which transcends all understanding, will guard your hearts and your minds in Christ Jesus."
~Philippians 4:6-7

Have you ever learned a "love lesson?" One of those lessons that can only be taught through true love and experience. This kind of lesson can never be learned during lust. "Love lessons" are very tough lessons to learn. It's more than just an emotional roller coaster. It breaks down all "walls" in every form. It completely exposes every part of who you are. It forces you to be accountable, to care, to respect things you never thought that you could tolerate. It forces you to look at things optimistically again. It leads you to speak to both the hurt and hope of the person you truly love. It helps you to put your faith into perspective. Love lessons reignite your prayer life. It revives your creativity. It gives you calm and inner peace. It helps you to see Corinthians 12 in the physical form. You ultimately become love yourself rather than simply chasing love to fill empty voids. The two of you become well connected.

Often, you may even find yourself rehearsing or rethinking your decisions. So many times, we forget to pray first and decide after. At times life can be so confusing. Time, love, and loyalty are much greater gifts than sex and those that are materialistic in nature. An even greater gift is that of motivation, wisdom, and the means to build a foundation that can secure a promising future. There many times is no way for another to see life through your lens. Instead, you must tell your story. It's one which is very beautiful, to say the least. Your story has also been impacted by many intersections of pain, hurt, and hardship. I'm sure that there were many tear-filled days, but guess what? You survived!

In relationships individuals hate being placed in the same category with "the others," but many tend to lead the pack in completing the same vicious, disloyal, confusing, manipulative, and emotionally abusive actions. Autumn's lover Alex was one of them. Selfishly, he continued for years to manipulate her into believing that he had her best interests at heart. As they conversed regularly, he realized how valuable her intimate thoughts were. Alex capitalized off Autumn's hurt, pain, emptiness, and insecurities. He pretended to be there for her; doing minor things and appearing in her corner as a supporter. He was nothing more than a snake. Thankfully the one that entered the picture last helped Autumn realize that Alex was not the only one capable of being so thoughtful, charming, supportive, focused, driven, and ambitious.

The new guy was the most genuine. Bryson came exuding confidence with a hint of humility. The intensity that existed between the two of them slowly and steadily began to eliminate the rest of her past from her emotional tank. The cologne that use to heighten Autumn's senses with pleasure suddenly had no impact at all. Bryson became that one that was different from all the rest. He was the only one that seemed to acknowledge and reward the value and positive impact of his woman. It was as if he'd found a way to listen to the more important things. He valued things that no other man had in her past. Bryson found value, solutions, and still could make a woman feel fulfilled even in his physical absence. He topped his hard work off with passion, drive, and care. Those characteristics were exactly what Autumn envisioned but always seemed to be missing in every dead-end relationship she found herself in.

The intersection of Professional, Family, and Mental Health:
As she reflected on her past business and personal relationships, she realized that each of her relationships invoked a past trauma somehow. When Autumn lost her first job to a company restructuring, she was mentally confronted with flashbacks of the morning drive that she took on the day that she lost her mother to cancer. The memory that flashed before her mentally launched her back into her 1996 green Nissan Sentra. She recalled herself driving to her summer gig listening to the gospel song "You saved me." She was driving on I 76; a two-lane area of the highway located in Pennsylvania. As she drove on that dreadful day;

Autumn found herself a great distance from North Philly. She was nestled between Conshohocken, Plymouth Meeting, and King of Prussia which are popular areas just outside of Philadelphia. During the drive; Autumn was praying to GOD that he would either take her mother and her pain away or heal her mother instantly and completely. She wanted GOD to do anything for her mother except allow her suffering to continue.

Eyes filled with tears, they poured down her cheeks, praying loudly in the car alone; she saw the skies appear to open. The sight was surreal. The colors were different hues of oranges, yellows, reds, blues, and pinks. This beautifully crafted masterpiece that GOD created appeared between the clouds before her tear-filled eyes. Autumn began to reflect on the many times that GOD saved her mother from death. She counted nine instances in which her mother had been given merciful chances. At that moment she realized that this was it. She went through an array of emotions but realized that this time it was her mother's turn to be called home and gain her heavenly wings. How does one go through so many stages of grief in an instance? As she drove into work; GOD gave her the acceptance that she later found out would help to support her entire family in their time of grieving and funeral planning.

Autumn never understood why after each different type of loss she was confronted with flashbacks of the day her mother died, but it happened, and it occurred frequently. Sometimes she believed that the flashbacks were with her because they helped and encouraged her not to give up. It's as if they're constant reminders that you lost someone you never thought you'd be able to live without, but you survived. If you could survive something so devastating, traumatic, and challenging as losing your mother then why would you not be able to survive and build after any other loss. Each time Autumn thought she'd lost big; she worked her ass off and gained even bigger. This is all due to the winner that lies within her. Autumn was the winner that her mother gave birth to and introduced the world to.

Autumn had very few words if she did not know or trust you. Assertive when necessary and passionate about those she loved.

Trying with everything in her to change the trajectory of her life from descending to ***Ascension***. She wrecked her brain daily trying to figure out how to make her life take off like the nightly flights she takes to different countries to maintain her relationship. Naturally, she presents a certain level of threat to the insecure in corporate America and those within the social service agencies. Autumn's smile lit up a room and her humble spirit drew authentic people to her. Her sense of style and class called for compliments, and her work ethic gained its merit. She had a genuine kindness which urged in others a desire to respect and appreciate her. Down to earth, free-spirited, world traveler, brains and beauty, and a grand authenticity that just could not be bought by competition. She was too mature to even notice the wicked actions and words of the immature. She received words of encouragement daily from her elders who more than anything wanted to live to see her win.

<u>Personal/ Social/ Intimate Health</u>
The first night with her lover had her thoughts all over the place. Excitement turned to, what did I get myself into? Which then turned to; I'm not into you, which turned to damn baby I didn't know that you had this in you? She went from peeking into the shower allowing her thoughts about being with him to go sour; to him enjoying every single drop of her. This led to him damn near devouring her just after his shower. With all the passion and care, he showed; her natural juices were released in less than an hour. The continuous sensual actions allowed her to temporarily be free of all the stresses she'd suppressed while she waited for his release, embrace, and arrival. Mind racing thought replacing, tongue chasing, good GOD he just replaced "him." I never knew that I'd be so into you. How and why is your tongue so wet, cool, warm, and hot at the same damn time? Just the right amount to creep up and touch her "G" spot. The sex was more than just hot. It was something that hit her soft and tender spot.

In just a few short minutes he made her forget it all. I mean… she'd already risked it all. He promised that through it all; he'd protect her from any unwanted harm or fall. He'd managed in his silence and only speaking through his sexual action to touch and remove every insecurity with his tongue. In just a few short minutes he had her sprung. All that time they'd spent probing one another; little did she know that chase would easily be replaced once she allowed him to get a sweet little taste. Initially not realizing, but there was a glimmer of opportunity that she chased. There was a gap that she wanted to fulfill which could never be replaced. She'd gone from being little Mrs. Perfect to her legs and nose being blown wide open. There was nothing that she wouldn't do for him. She allowed him to talk her into breaking all her most cherished rules for him.

How could something that started so innocent turn into something that could be so passionate? Only for it to lead to something so desperate. From the nightclubs to the random trips to NYC he made sure to keep her in atmospheres that she never realized she would appear in! She'd be a vixen in the evening and a blue-collar worker by day. Mrs. Bright in the night and losing sight by day. Her nose was so open that she just had to inflict all this action on someone. Leaning on the one woman in the office whose life was perceived to be more than a little hectic. She'd swap stories about her long nights and early morning's; always emphasizing how much she'd adored him. Little did she know; in just a few short months life would leave the two of them scorn. Over time she managed to disassociate the intrusive, deceptive, and greedy behaviors that would have sent anyone with sense "red flags."

As Autumn recalls this relationship, she couldn't help but think of her very first mental health client case. She was assigned a battered incarcerated female. She completed her first behavioral assessment on the battered female. She had no idea that years later that this woman's direct experience was the perfect depiction of what she would be confronted with. The horrific description of her clients experiences explained her internal torment so well. If the story were written- it would read as follows: As the iron heats up along with the argument, hurtful words fly back and forth between the two and eventually' he blows a fuse. His words burn similar to the way her clients back burned from the hot iron. Skin sizzling like fried sunny side up egg on a restaurant grill as he raged. As things intensify so does the nerves throughout her body. She called out for help to the lord above while dialing 9-1-1.

Numerous disagreements, the first and second instances in which he put his hands on her. The lies, manipulation, and a multitude of females that he entertained. Could you imagine putting so much trust into someone? Autumn's first thought was believing that her partner would only protect her and never hurt nor neglect her. The devastation she'd experience was shocking after the first strike. Trapped in her apartment thinking that this would be the end of her days. Her first instinct was to call the police. He immediately snatched the phone from her hands and out of the wall. She was frightened. When she attempted to check her face for bruises or deformity caused by his hands; he stood in front of her. She explained that she needed to use the bathroom. He followed her. She pleaded with him for permission to look in the mirror. He stood over her. She proceeded to leave the bathroom. He blocked and questioned her. She explained that she wanted to lay down. He followed her. She sat on the bed. He sat close to her staring at her. She laid down to go to sleep. He sat up all night watching her. She woke up the next morning to prepare for work. He prevented her from leaving. She begged him to allow her to go to work. He forced her to call out.

He knew not to allow her to leave his sight as she would have too much access to the police. She called in to speak with her supervisor and asked to work from home. Her supervisor made an allowance for her. She pulled out her laptop. He monitored her. He did not miss an email sent, a document opened, or word typed. This was the longest day of her life. He silently built up fear in her. He forced her to have sex with him. She laid limp. He grew frustrated. That did not stop him from completing the entire act. He finally finished. Tears rolled down her cheeks. She laid there silently and helpless. Never in a million years did she ever think this would happen to her. She was embarrassed. Days later after the swelling went down from her eyes and face; she was allowed to go to work.

While at work she was questioned as to why she was wearing sunglasses in office. She was too embarrassed and afraid to tell. She made up a story about possibly having the "pink eye" so that she could leave the office early. When she finally went to the hospital, she found out that she had a busted vein in her eye and some minor retinal damage that could be cured by steroid eye drops and oral medications. She learned that during the encounter; she had a silent asthma attack. She thought that she'd come up with the best lie to tell the medical staff at her doctor's office, but there was one who could not keep his thoughts to himself. She proceeded to tell him that she fell and hit her eye on the edge of her bed, and he replied "really?" "Do you expect me to believe that?" "That's your story huh?" "Ok." "You're sticking to it?" "Whatever you say." She felt some type of way, but she had no time to complain as her abuser sat waiting in the car for her to finish with her medical appointment.

When she finally mustered up enough guts to develop an exit plan to finally leave him; there was that one that made it all so very easy. No fight. Just full cooperation. No resistance. Simple go with the flow type of behavior. One that you could trust to be exactly who he introduced you to. One of the sexiest things that a man can do is to try something new that his woman introduces him to. Some don't realize how much they miss out on by being so resistant to change, honest attempts at being spontaneous, and freeing yourself enough to take full advantage to truly live life. It's time to break out of the prison of pain. Remember that **YOU** are no good to anyone "looked up." Many fool themselves into believing that strength is in holding on, but there are times when the strength is in letting go.

She gives thanks to the one that opened her eyes and not just her nose. She quickly learned to appreciate him. His truth was the best and sexiest thing that he exposed her to. He had no idea how much her mind, desire to focus, confidence, and a hint of what others may have perceived as arrogance did for her. It was as if she finally realized that it was all right to stand out. He always found a way even in silence to show her through his actions that she deserved more. He found a way to help her realize that the boundaries she'd set were indeed justified. He complimented her both silently and verbally. It was as if he knew all the answers to her questions without her parting her lips to ask. He lifted a burden from her shoulders without making her feel guilty for needing help. The experiences he presented were nothing short of true depictions of elevated intensity and real love.

Excitedly as she invited him in; although she had no idea how the rest of her night would begin or end. She laid back following his instructions. Staring into his eyes which were filled with seduction. As he gripped her legs, caressed, and pulled them toward him; her mind began to race. She began to feel his sweet and tender embrace as his tongue traced her laced covered cupcake. He began his intake. Never making even the slightest mistake. She rested with her eyes closed as she lay there completely exposed and allowed him to have total control.

He ate her cupcake so well she quivered trying her best to gently exhale. Her legs shaking as he continues to kiss and suck; man, he really had her stuck. She tried to pull away, but bae wanted to have her his way. As he touched on her curves and way; in her mind, she wanted to make him stay. The crazy part about that was; he only came to play but could not even think about an overnight stay. Nonetheless, she served that cupcake up as if it was brought out to him on a restaurant tray, but the way that he devoured her little flower left her legs too weak to even walk to her shower. The meeting of the minds did not last an hour. Although this was not their first interaction; he left a very memorable impression. He made his statement in ways she could never tear apart. He ended up singing to her beautiful heart.

A few meetings in and he had yet to disappoint. He showed up each time making a better impression than the last. They both knew that regardless of whether they conversed, played, or got laid; ultimately, they'd end up having a blast. She soon realized that life nor relationships had to be difficult. Long term or honeymoon phase all could be well played. She longed to spend many nights with him, but she knew that approach never worked out in the past. If she learned nothing else from past relationships; she learned not to move too fast. Yet and still she seemed to make one huge mistake which reminded her of her past. She slept with him too soon, but still did not regret giving up the jazz.

Spiritual/ Religious Health:

When is the last time you have searched for answers through prayer, fasting, focus in the confines of your religious covering? There is not one person on this earth that is perfect, not one book written that has all the answers to the world's problems. As long as you are aware that there is a presence of love and covering greater than yourself; you can be reassured that whatever decision you make GOD will see you through. If you are not doing so already; **Pause** for one moment here and reflect. From this point forward allow yourself to receive constructive criticism from within as this will help guide you in determining the changes you need to make as you move forward. Without beating yourself up; take a moment to reflect and accept GOD's most precious gifts of grace and mercy as you're continuously covered. Allow yourself to become your inner Autumn. Lift your head high removing all disguise; allowing yourself to be as transparent as possible while GOD supplies. It's time for you to remove yourself from people, places, and things that no longer serve or grow you. This can be the day you finally wake up and feel empowered enough to say, "it's time for me to walk away because this situation is no longer serving the current or future me." Make yourself aware of this FACT- If it's not motivating you then it does not deserve you.

Financial Health and its impact on intimacy/ love:

Nestled between he loves being with being, loves occasionally hanging out with me, loves doing nice things for me, but why is it that I was not good enough for him to propose and marry me? At a time when you're trying to find out if you want to be married or if you only want to be a part of the fancy proposal and matching outfits trend? You realize that you must put your life into perspective and quickly.

If a man falls for a woman for the mere fact that she presents herself impeccably well daily, is able to clearly and confidently articulate herself, and has what it takes to join him in the empire he's building; then why the heck can't she make her own money, increase her value, as well as the expectations she has for her man?

Thoughts of being showered with expensive gifts, high-end shoes, and handbags; only to flaunt for others and hear them brag of her fab and swag. If only she knew that all he had was a few cute rags and one trash bag to grab. Growing tired of fighting during frequent behavioral fires she aspires to fulfill her desires. Desires to move on with someone filled with ambition and a will to live free of avenues that lead to grave sights and brick walls lined with barbed wire was what she truly wanted to transpire. Sometimes we are in so much pain, so much want, and so much of self that we fail to realize the predicaments GOD places us in to gives us the ability to realize what we need. Many times, things that we feel are breaking us are healing and rebuilding us. For the first time, Autumn realized how much she was truly loved. She even realized her faults. She realized much of her very own failure was exactly what she constantly projected on him. She was finally able to take accountability for her brokenness. She realized that as much as she felt she was communicating; all she'd been doing was talking. He listened and respected her silence. He was changing for love. He was meeting all her requests, but because she wanted to hurriedly fix both their financial positions; she unknowingly overlooked his progress.

Sometimes as individuals we allow outside factors to dictate our sense of urgency. Many times, as we rush to catch up and or surpass those that we feel have already "arrived." In turn, we hurt our future and the one you love most. We must stop allowing outside forcing to put cracks in our foundations built on love and faith. Stop going to social media and materialistic things for validation. Focus, be consistent, apply what you have learned, take advantage of every positive opportunity, quietly, and steadily move into your purposeful position in GOD's timing. For you never know why your timing has been slowed. It could be all so that you can reset and gain a new momentum that becomes you're sure shot at the next level. Here's an Autumn fact; she has trust issues. Oh, don't act like you haven't struggled with them yourself. If one were to play by the rules of "the dating game" they would tell you that everyone he or she has ever trusted caused the same types of hurt, pain, resentment, and disappointment. Family, friends, coworkers, employers, mentors, and lovers have done strange things that cause pain. It's for that reason; trust and loyalty are so hard to come by. That does not mean that one cannot trust. Nor does it mean that one cannot love. It just means that those who have been through betrayal are not as eager to be taken advantage of a second time. They are no longer interested in wearing regret. People have their agendas. Some make sacrifices based on the position and lifestyles they desire. People will build an empire with one person only to leave for another.

Distrust is a learned from layers of experiences that are sometimes devastated by disappointments and despair. Many are learning to discover whether they are the agenda, prize, chosen one, or if they are just the stepping stool. One can realize that they have evolved when they no longer have an attraction to the things and people that have destroyed them in the past.

Heartfelt letters and verbal professions of love is just not enough for someone who has completely healed. No one gets to have you without putting the correct, legit, and well thought out actions into play. No more making it easy for anyone especially when life and love have been so tough to grasp. The one that you love may not be looking to make you suffer. If you have wronged him or her in the past and want your lover to be present in your future - you're going to have you work for it and prove yourself beyond a reasonable doubt.

If the lover has elevated and healed; he or she will not allow the priceless and rare jewel that they have become to be marked down or made easily available to you or anyone else for that matter. We all reach our "done" points. This is the point in one's life in which you are through going "through." You become tired of focusing on the wrong nonsense. Tired of telling people what you want. Greed and manipulation come in so many different forms. Regardless of what your story or position is; be determined not to live a life scorned. I challenge you to treat yourself like a new or potential customer. Begin to allow yourself to have an abundance of options in every area of your life. Especially in your finances. This way you will become a hot commodity and not some underrated push over.

Chapter 3: The Reality of Running
Proverbs 17:22 "A merry heart does good, like medicine, but a broken spirit dries the bones."

She is not sure... For that reason alone; she runs... Runner's take your marrrrrrk's, seeeeet, bomb! (the starter's pistol goes off).

"Running" leads to loneliness. Many times, you want to reach out to loved ones and friends, but there is a part of you that asked yourself- should I return to the people that bring me the most anxiety, uncertainty, and judgment or am I better off alone? Night after night, she laid alone. Autumn moved four states away to free her loved ones of any contact with her faults.

Family, Mental, and Physical Health
Come here, have a seat, get some rest, you are tired; her mother gently says to her. Even though mom is battling cancer and most likely tired herself; she could still sense the pain, fear, and fact that she had been watching her daughter run from the reality of losing her. Trips to the beach, frequent family outings, gatherings, and constant visitors could never tame the beast lurking amongst her family in the name of loss and cancer. With mom tired from the cancer treatments, pain vibrating through her joints, muscles, bones, and uncertainty of whether her children would be alright given she'd been preparing for her final blessed flight; she stayed strong maintaining her position of love and strength.

On a beautiful day in August, mom would be freed from her battle with cancer. Pain shooting through her body like a million volts of power which could illuminate more than a watchtower. Grandma had slept on the long sofa that night only a glass divider separating mother and child by only three feet. Grandma's instructions were for her daughter's child to head to bed, which separated another mother and child by a stairwell and six feet. Reluctantly she'd followed her grandmother's instructions and went to her room, only to crawl into bed to hear her mother's cries well into the night. As her mother cried Autumn wept and prayed. The pain displayed in different forms and different areas of the house. She'd promised herself that if mom was still crying out for help in the morning; she would not leave for work. Autumn would instead stay home to keep her mom company as she fought through what she felt was her mother's final fight.

It was four-thirty in the morning when her alarm sounds. As the alarm goes off, she hears her mother's cries. Determined to be present by her mother's bedside; she rises from the bed and moves toward the stairs to be with her mother. As she quietly begins to walk down the stairs, only reaching the 6th step from the top; her grandmother instructs her to get ready for work. Although she insisted that she wanted to be with her mother; her grandmother asserted herself and sternly ordered her to "do as I say." Although hesitant, she ascends the stairs. Upset and wanting to disobey the recent order; she proceeded up the stairway to prepare for work. She then showered, brushed her teeth, and sloppily slipped on her clean work uniform. Usually, she would take pride in getting dressed. Her clothes were typically pressed, her blouse would be buttoned to the top, her pants would fit perfectly, and her tie would be neatly tied. Not this time. Pain would not allow it.

This particular morning was different. Autumn felt as though she knew what would soon transpire in just a matter of hours. Her body fatigued, mind racing, and emotions were all over the place. Resentful of her grandmother's orders; she kissed her mother and left the house. She closed the door with a gut feeling that this would be the last time that she'd see her mother alive. Remaining optimistic, she hoped for the best. She walked to her car, unlocking the driver side door to her 1996 four-door green Nissan Sentra and sat in the driver seat. Shoes untied, shirt barely buttoned, and running slightly behind her ideal leave time for work. She sat still in her driver seat with her driver side door wide open, and car keys in her hand instead of the ignition.

Frustrated that there was nothing she could do to make her mother's pain go away. Sad because of the grim reality that her mother could die while she was at work. Still she proceeded as she needed. As she drove to work praying, crying, frustrated with her current circumstances, and confused as to what GOD's plan for her mother's fate was; she continued to drive. With every mile closer to work yet farther away from her mother; the anxiety worsened. The pain cut deeper, and the uncertainty provided no relief to her. As strong of a young woman she was; she felt her life begin to fill with numerous cracks. Those cracks resembled the pain and breaking point she was facing as she thought of life without her mother.

Have you ever realized that everything you've set out to build, revitalize, or attempted to cure in others; is the very thing that you need to take time to address within yourself? There are too many broken individuals trying to heal their brokenness while using others as their guinea pigs and financial footstools. Studies show that people in vulnerable positions are the easiest targets. Let's take an individual who isn't doing so great financially, for instance; perhaps they've suffered a job loss or had a recent financial hardship. They're more likely to be a victim of "get rich quick" schemes, willing to take criminal risks, and even become prey to predatory lenders.

Autumn was continually trying to heal every man that she dated. What she failed to realize was that she continuously put a terrible physical and emotional beaten on herself. Each time one healed, they became strong enough to leave her, pursue, and marry someone else. Never sure as to whether each of them knew that they added to her preexisting traumas that she'd struggled with; she was determined not to become a bitter female. She continued to believe that love was a possibility for her. What she could not understand was why it was so hard? Why did she have to always prove herself to the man she gave her love too? Why were life and relationships never easy for her? She felt that no matter the type of man she dated; she met resentment, adversity, emptiness, and avoidance.

Autumn had been through so much in her life that she developed the ability to mentally and emotionally escape, even when she could not physically do so. Just when she'd gotten the urge to run again; she'd talked herself into a final visit. Uncertain of the outcome; she hoped for the best result possible; no matter which way the pendulum swung. Plagued by stress, fear, uncertainty, and anxiety; she felt things were getting off to a great start. Within hours of her arrival, the enemy planted a passive seed of sadness. The sadness transferred to her as stress and aggression from him. Soon she understood what attributed to the sudden mood change. She grew flustered, fed up, and almost willing to walk away from all that she loved. Instead, he caught her vibe and made it very clear that he was ready to step up and win with her. He fought for her love. He assertively informed her that she wasn't going anywhere. His ears, eyes, and heart were all open for her to see for the very first time. She finally saw for herself that he loved her. She no longer needed to ask him how he felt about her. She saw it in his actions. She finally realized that he was learning how to treat her.

For so many years he was figuring it all out on his own. No one to turn to for help. No one in his corner. No one was willing to go the extra mile. No mentors or male figures that could help him understand what it took and meant to love a woman properly. All because no one ever thought that they should take the initiative to be there for him. All he knew was how to be there for everyone else. He had not experienced much help from anyone, especially not a female having his best interests at heart. He didn't understand her "fight" for him. He initially saw her as being overbearing, controlling, and too aggressive. He had no idea that those traits and behaviors were actual displays and purposeful actions, which clearly illustrated how she loved. All she knew was how to protect, build, and to think for others. Her frustrations grew for him because she was looking for someone who could finally come along and direct her. On this one trip in particular; it all clicked for both of them. He finally realized that it was best that he began to take the initiative. For once in their relationship, he realized that it was ok for him to take the lead.

As she began to look closer in the mirror at her triggers; she realized he was presently experiencing similar traumas. Being the woman, she was, she wanted to protect him from those dangers, threats, and setbacks. Whenever she saw that someone was even remotely close to attempting any action that resembled something that she experienced in her past, but on him; she, in turn, went into attack mood. She would verbally warn him. When he did not take heed to her warning, she would grow frustrated with him. Whenever the outcome was the exact result that she expected; she lost that much more respect for those that committed the manipulative actions.

Constant frustrations, learned lessons, and elevated loved for him had her constantly raising questions. Over time she noticed that he stopped confiding in her. She perceived that as disloyal, sneaky, and inconsistent behavior. One day he informed her that "it's not that I don't trust you or want to tell you stuff; it's just that I know how you get." Curiously, she asked, ``How do I get?" He explained, you react and are always ready to snap. Confusion filled her mind. Everything that she felt internally were visibly displayed in body language and on her face. The genuine concern, heartful, and instinctive reaction from a woman wanting to protect her man from the pain she once felt was overwhelming and unwelcomed. Being raised by so many single females who were continually protecting their sons; Autumn finally realized that she had not learned how to "stay in a woman's place." She finally realized that there comes a time where you must allow him to figure it out. You must give him time to go through the same range of emotions that you've experienced. You must allow him to kick the habit. You can help, but only where he opens the door to his feelings and invite you in. You cannot force yourself into someone else's stages of grief, loss, or story for that matter.

She learned this after ending a shackled relationship that set her accomplishments back ten years. Drained her savings accounts, depleted 401k's, tarnished credit scores, threatened professional licenses, increased debt, and was met with heartbreak; is what chasing love once got her. She, in turn, allowed herself to develop a passion for self. Once she made that change, things began to take its rightful place; just as she did. Initially, she looked at those failed relationships and the destruction aimed at her professional character as regrets, but now she sees them as the progressive steps. Although hurtful at the time; she managed to overcome the same adversities that she attempted to avoid but ended up having to face.

Frequent counseling visits to help with one area, but the topic of discussion remained the same. The thing that concerned Autumn most was her relationship. She was in love but trying to avoid it. She hurt for him and was filled with so much resentment because although it was family that had his attention; she could not stand the fact that another woman had so much control over his emotions and finances. She hated it. She wanted to extinguish anyone that caused him harm. She was a fighter and runner. When she felt or sensed any pain or negativity; she would immediately remove herself from its path. Her frustration developed in her relationship because she wanted to remove him from the pain path as well, but it seemed he desired to stand in the line of fire. She could not stand it!

While in therapy Autumns therapist asked her, are you willing to accept him where he is and for who he is right now? Autumn responded; I believe I can. She wanted them to stop hurting and draining him. In her mind, each time that he gave them his last; it took away from their present and future as a couple. He is a man with a kind heart and a weakness for ensuring that children are adequately nurtured. He never wants to see a child (especially one that he loves) hurting, starving, or wishing for anything. She felt the same. She does not respect adults who use children as pawns to get what they want. She finally realized that she grew flustered with his situation because she was still experiencing some of the same pains and challenges herself. She felt that she was able to put some healthy boundaries in place that he had not yet achieved. She was more willing to discuss her concerns, hardships, and plans with him. She felt slighted when he refused to share. She did not realize she had been passing judgment on him while allowing her issues to go unaddressed. So often this is the case for individuals with a history of trauma. Traumatized individuals project past traumas on those that are closest to them.

Playing keep away, blocking a contact, walking away, moving away, or lashing out are nothing more than bandages. In Autumn

Ascension

mind, she thought of those approaches as significant safety measures and concrete solutions. The problem was that she never actually addressed the trauma associated with each incident. In turn, it was putting a bad verbal and emotional beating on the man she loved. She wanted him to improve and eliminate things that she had not even correctly personally addressed. She was projecting all of her emotions on him given she looked to him for peace and safety. She felt as though others were infiltrating their peace and joy zone. She wanted out for both herself and the man she loved.

Autumn kept wondering to herself; how is it that when I am at work, I can handle things in a calmer, healthier, and strength-based manner, but when I am at home, I am quick to anger. She realized that her work behaviors are better because any lack of professionalism means disciplinary actions which could eliminate her paycheck. Money and business were of value to her. She then questioned herself. How is that you have put more merit on people and uncertainty than you do on the man that you love and who loves you? She came to this conclusion shortly after she told him that she does not want to be with a man who does not make her a priority. In her mind, we are preparing for a future together and if she is not a priority now then she would not be one in the future.

One will be damned if you will be taking food out of our families mouths to feed someone else who was being irresponsible with their finances and daily activities. She felt as though it was one thing to feed someone in need which fell on hard times (job loss, sickness, extenuating circumstance), but another to help someone who chooses to spend their funds on unnecessary shopping sprees while expecting another to clean up the mess that they made. You must be honest with yourself and realize when you cannot afford to take care of or help others. Aiding others is a lovely gesture, but you cannot put yourself in a hole while doing so. You must support and build yourself before helping others. For if you cannot save yourself, how can you save anyone else?

Certain things need to be reserved for GOD. JUDGMENT is one of them. We do it all the time, whether consciously or subconsciously, but we do it. Instances where we want to start, we must first take the time to fully reflect on some of our own decisions and proceed with caution. If we would do this often; this can and will decrease our likelihood to point out the logs or flaws in the eyes or lives of others. By no means am I advising you to fund someone else's fault. I am, however, suggesting that you proceed with caution and pray much more than you respond. The cautious approach will help you to keep your relationship with yourself, family, partner, lover, friends, professionals, and GOD in a better and much healthier place.

You must keep in mind that there will be instances where you can have rational thoughts. In the same token, life sometimes will throw a wrench in both your plans and emotions. It will be at that point that you will be responsible for exercising mental, physical, and emotional control. Life will send you disappointments and great experiences. It will be up to you to make the best out of everything. To make the best means to stay positive for every opportunity, pitiful, blessing, gift, and challenge. Do not allow circumstances or people to control your moods. What you think is what you become. Remember, both growth and patience are necessary.

Self- Inventory

Give yourself a few minutes to complete the self-inventory below:

What do you want from yourself?

1._____

Are you generally happy or sad?

2._____

Do you feel hopeful or hopeless?

3._____

Do you feel bond or free?

4._____

Do you feel you have what it takes to achieve your goals?

5._____

How much time are you giving yourself to achieve your goals?

6._____

How much effort have you put into your goals, passion, and purpose?

7._____

Chapter 4: Critical Moments
F.O.E- Faith Over Everything

Autumn was continuously internalizing everything and never speaking to anyone. Autumn was always helping everyone and feeling like she has been walking around with blinders. Head hung as low as her self- esteem. Posture completely wrong. Blinded by love, hurt, pain, and stress; she realized that it was time to buckle down and level up. She needed to get right with GOD first and foremost. Secondly, she needed to pay more attention to herself. Lastly, it was indeed time to hustle like never before.

You may feel that you are constantly going through a storm. Understand this; this passing storm is one designed for those who want more. Know that the level that you have been praying for is obtainable. GOD is preparing you for your blessing. You will be tested, humbled, cracked, but not broken. Those challenges will repair and prepare you to weather future storms and not be phased, blindsided, or surprised by them. Leaders must know how to teach, train, communicate, and complete the tasks that they want efficiently and effectively executed. Do not be discouraged. Do not give up. Step up to your come up!

In business; hard decisions are inevitable. At times the hard decision can be between choosing to hire one fantastic candidate over another. The opposing side is that you may have to decide between letting go of one of your more talented employees over the other. As an employee; Autumn tried her best to focus on the positive that was in leadership. She always envisioned herself as a leader. She focused mostly on learning from genuine and intelligent leaders while internally dismissing the actions of those that were rude, condescending, and disrespectful.

The most frustrating part of life is when it seems as though time is not on your side in any situation. It does not matter if it is within your relationship, work, or life in general. When life seems to be handing you bad apples, you do not always think to make apple cider. When life throws you lemons of every form; you may not always have a taste for lemonade. When it appears as though the joke is on you; you may not even think to have a parade. One thing that she had been known to do; no matter the obstacle; she always continued to PUSH through. There has never been any good coming out of giving up. As they say in basketball- the only bad shot is the one not taken.

Stop sitting around, waiting on your blessings, and start seeking them out. You are no use to anyone confined, stagnant, suppressed, silent, or locked up. You must build a solid foundation. Such a foundation must be assembled on systems, time management, structure, focus, finances, and execution. In business, you must be personable, but never get personal. Keep your eyes open, use your best judgment, and do not fall victim to failed research. Know both your business and private numbers. You should know the statistics of the companies you work for, your future competition, and the company that you plan to own. When the opportunity presents itself; capitalize off all that your employers have to offer. Allow your current employers to finance your future. Know that to gain; you must start somewhere. Be employable, employed, and have experience in employing to understand the entire process. This way, you learn what it took to obtain, attain, and retain employment and business assets.

You must know the difference between proof of concept and execution. There is also a difference between a pitch and a detailed plan. Knowing the details becomes the difference between a sample piece of cake and the entire recipe. For you; this means the difference between being self-employed and building an empire. You want to give the consumer enough to desire to buy, but never enough to fire you from your dream because they now have your entire recipe. Remember, everyone is hungry, whether it is for food, money, luxury, fame, attention, or emotional reciprocity.

As you move and make progress at some point, you must lose all that is holding you back, including the person that you use to be. Do not allow your past to drive you mad. You must enable your future desires to inspire you to do more. This mindset will expedite you to the highest point in your future. Understand that who you are today will not be who you are years, months, or days from now. Know that we live and function in a system of money. It's time that you understand your heritage. What type of business trader are you? Are you a trader of goods, services, currency, talent, or systems?

Understand that everything you expose yourself to; creates an experience. Every experience can generate a new idea. Every new idea can generate a new approach. Every new approach can create a new income stream. You must become a problem solver in all that you do. The ability to problem solve applies to every area of life. Life will present you with many adversities, trials, tragedies, and challenges; you have to P.U.S.H (Pray Until Something Happens) through. There will be instances in which you believe that you have figured it all out. The moment that you reach that point a new challenge surfaces. You cannot fear change, but instead, you must embrace it. You must step up to the plate and act. You are not allowed to sleep on it. Life will beat you down at times, but you must rely on your inner survivor.

Many times, life will not allow time for breaks, vacations, or rest when you are striving to achieve your goals. You must stay ready, continue planning, and always executing. You cannot fix your mind on going back. Instead, you must focus on getting out of your current position. Life can frequently feel like a constant battle with many losses, but you must appreciate both the small and large wins. Never stall. Keep pushing through it all.

Seven areas of Mental Business:
Your body is your business

Product:
Understanding that you are your product. You must ensure that you remain the best most cutting edge, most innovative, and most decent human being on the market. Always be ready to beat the odds. For your potential client or customer to trust you; you must be willing, confident, and able to trust yourself. You must be able to stand the test of time. You cannot just be a part of a fade. You

must remain timeless, attractive, solution-based, focused, and resilient. You must be able to understand your specialty market, be aware that it is always time to train, study, and refresh. You also need to know when you need to reevaluate your approach entirely. You must understand that times change, as well as people and industries. There will come a time in your life where you will have to redesign your thought process. Your image and your blueprint will also need adjustments. To achieve the levels that you are striving for; changes are best. That time is likely to be NOW!

Process:

As an individual looking not merely to sustain self, but to create a sense of freedom, you must learn and understand the need associated with self-organization and coordination. Many times, we are trying to ensure that we have enough income flowing to secure our bills and financial wellbeing. On the other hand; we miss the need for peace and positivity. So much effort is put forth to be better contributors to our professional lives. We tend to forget the importance of consistency in allowing healthy foods to flow into our bodies. Replenish every bit of energy that flows out. For instance, after you have worked all day, you need adequate sleep at night. After you have poured love into your relationship and family, you must give some love to self. Keep people around you that are willing to replenish what has flown out of you and into them.

For every ounce of energy burned during physical activity and fitness routines, you must put the right foods back into your body to sustain your physical health. You must be a complete and finished product before you can lend yourself to anyone or anything else. In addition to core functions of what it takes to be who you are, you must expose yourself to a wide variety of routines, services, activities, and business ventures. That will help you with all your specific needs as to not expose yourself to losses of any kind. The more that you grow in business, you become more susceptible to human vultures of every kind. As you elevate, there will be others that have trouble assimilating to your success.

That said, be sure to cover yourself and your business legally, financially, with real estate, and all other areas that are pertinent to maintain your successes.

Organizational:

There's a saying in business and it goes as follows: *It is so much easier to eat an elephant one bite at a time than to try to eat the entire elephant at once.* For you to achieve the level of prestige that you desire in your professional area, you will need to be able to hold yourself accountable. You must either have someone that can serve as a supervisor to your productivity or be extremely disciplined yourself. You must have an excellent handle on your value and self-worth. Ensure that you are not holding yourself back because you are the only one underestimating your capabilities. There are people around you who are not as educated, or talented as you, but they ascended. The difference is that they remained consistent, confident, and hungry enough to take the risks that you continue to avoid.

Strategy:

You must have a plan of action. It does not matter whether you are trying to come up with a plan to sustain your family or if you are working to create and build a brand. You need to establish and continue to build on the relationships that you have developed. Active links are essential with your customers, vendors, within your organization, and even your family. Where there is a happy, thriving family unit; you will find a successful individual and business. You may not realize the impact that your personal life has on your business and social life, but it is significant. Keeping positive energy from the time that you wake up in the morning until you lay in bed at night is important. Influencing customers and prospective buyers to continue to invest in or purchase your goods and services all lead back to the need to stay positive and personable.

Technology:

It is one thing to know how to use technology and another to understand why or how to make it work to profit your business. It is truly extraordinary when you can be the system within your business. Systems promote information and communication usage within and outside of your company. Data and technology increase your company's visibility and all the excellent services available to prospective clients. Do not be afraid to be technical, specific, or critical as you need to understand all the details within you and your business.

Marketing:
Establish a healthy home foundation to be your most focused and creative self. It can be tough to come up with unique and innovative marketing ideas when you are distracted by personal matters. One way to mentally approach this is by looking at who you are and what you are doing behind closed doors. As previously stated, remind yourself daily that your body is your brand. You must be careful with whom you associate yourself with, how you present yourself in public, and how you manage your home life. Know that everything you do can become a brand or business, but you must realize what you want your brand to represent. You must understand how to identify opportunities in the market. Effectively position your brand in such a way that the product gets introduced at the right time. Optimize the use of your customer or client base. From a business perspective, you always must be prepared to promote and deliver.

Service:
The disposition to always be willing, ready, and able to teach is the true epitome of service. There are so many that feel like they have made it, but are operating in selfishness. To be selfless is the greatest way to create a legacy in which your brand and you as the individual will be able to live past your lifetime. This has been proven time and time again. In recent times we can look at the legacy that was left behind with hip hop artist Nipsey Hussle. He was self-taught, he researched everything, and he was not afraid to teach others what he learned. Countless interviews, social events, and business transactions depicted him giving back. The most secure way to secure your brand is to make sure that your customers have your support along with the information they need. Please always and forever understand that the power remains with

the buyer. If you have not done so already and you plan to go into sales or service; educate yourself on the impact of supply and demand. Ensure customers have the support and information they need which will make them want to indulge in what your business has to offer. Business owners that support their communities most; maintain the support and loyalty from their fan base and customer.

Financial

We have all heard the phrase and most likely understand that money makes the world go around. Even during your business planning process, you must understand and be able to adequately elaborate on what it will take to start and operate your business. Get used to working within a budget even if you have never done so in the past. You must also be able to develop a budget for your business, especially if you plan on going to the banks to borrow money for start-up costs. I have provided a few helpful tips that will give you insight as you prepare to marry your business:

Avoid these business blunders

- Do not announce that you are doing something too early
- Do not use the products or pictures of other businesses on your site
- Do not conduct business with folks just because you know them
- Do not mix business with pleasure
- Do not quit your 9-5p too soon
- Treat yourself like a lender
- Cut out unnecessary bills
- Do not over purchase supplies or product

Do's of business

- Do your research
- Start an email list
- Stay loyal to your business (consistency is key)
- Get people to sign up for your mailing list
- Teach yourself to create things on your own
- Do business with companies that can back their product or service

- Never put more than 10-15% of the total cost of renovations out front in real estate
- Surround yourself with like-minded individuals and business owners
- Reinvest what you make from your business back into your business
- Save the same amount of money that you need to cover your personal and business expenses if you are thinking of leaving your job
  - Prove to yourself that you can sustain yourself for at least two years before leaving your full-time job

I come to you as humble as I know how when I say this. By no means are you ever to go into any business deals without a clearly defined signed and executed contract. You must take binding precautionary measures for yourself and future. Clear, specific, and detailed contracts will save you a great deal of time and money in the long run. Do NOT start any projects with any contractors without a clear blueprint, contract, itemized project budget, and full walkthrough. You have no idea how much time and effort you will be able to save yourself in the end. I discourage you from paying for things that you can do yourself. If you have the time, confidence, and experience to complete specific tasks; be sure to do so on your own.

Chapter 5: Evolve

A good person leaves an inheritance for their children's children, but a sinner's wealth is stored up for the righteous. ~Proverbs 13:22

Autumn would have so many intense conversations with herself. She would constantly question her actions and decisions. Questioning yourself is not a bad approach when you are trying to elevate. That said, let's take an opportunity to do some self-reflecting as we move forward.

Mental Health
Who are you? Are you becoming who you want to be? Are you open and excited about change?
One thing that you must keep in mind is that the only person you truly need to hold on to is you. Erykah Badu makes this known in her song "Bag Lady. "Evolving many times means getting a genuine handle on your emotions. It means not only having a hard exterior but at times having an even harder core. There are times when you will need to keep your game face displayed. You are not allowed to expose your true emotional positioning; especially in the beginning. Remain extremely focused. If you have a partner; you two have no time to be at odds as you must constantly stand on one accord — unity birth's empires. Jealousy and resentment have no place.

The same way that you learn what you like, love, and dislike; you begin to realize who you are, what you want, and precisely what it is that you truly deserve. You recognize what levels you are capable of soaring to and understand the lows that you never want to see. Life will present many challenges and much aggression, which will wake up assertiveness in even the shyest person. The experience will show you moments that make you question whether you can achieve your childhood or newfound goals. Ultimately it is up to you to never give up and to keep trying. Over the years, you will learn to realize that life, relationships, business ventures, and the person you are; are all one challenging marathon.

If you are not aware already; you will learn that you are not perfect. Conversely, you are indeed the ideal person assigned to take on the tasks beautifully presented to you. You have been designed perfectly to fulfill the purpose assigned to your life. There will be times in which you are uninvited or unprepared. The lesson here is to make those instances rare or nonexistent. There will be times where you have studied and feel well prepared but get to the main event and realize that what you expected does not exist. It will then be up to you to be able to present yourself as the resilient problem solver that you are. Always be ready to think quick, respond, be proactive, and seldom reactive. If you are only preparing for one moment; you will not be equipped for the millions of others that will present themselves to you. If you are continually thinking ahead, then you have a much better chance of staying ahead of the competition. All successful businesses, companies, and empires are being proactive in advance of 10 years. If you continue to be on the cutting edge of your profession; you will never become extinct.

As you begin to evolve; your thoughts, actions, approaches, and responses will change. There will be moments where you say to yourself; "had I not done this then I would be in a better place." There will also be instances in which you reflect and say to yourself, "Wow, I am happy to have overcome or bypassed that mishap." As one evolves the conversations, things, and people that you use to put so much time and effort in to begin to dissolve. Meaningless conversations and idling all become unattractive to you. Rehashes and rehearsals of your past that does not enhance your present or feed your future will even appall you. You will become less attracted to drama understanding that it impedes success and progress.

Most get caught at the interaction of what am I doing wrong, and what do I do next? Reassurance without having to ask is neccessary. Where's my motivation? How do I avoid the struggle? You will become tired of being fearful of job elimination raising its evil head. What's next? Who am I? Talented individuals grow tired of giving up all their intellectual property for such a low return on investment. Loyal professionals become tired of not being able to trust the people around them. Given we live and work in environments driven by the concept of "every man for themselves" while continually referring to the direct reports as "a team," you have to maintain multiple streams of income.

How do I get myself out of this? We all have done some things that we may regret or felt as though those experiences served as valuable lessons. Over time and in a perfect scenario, one would learn from the first blunder. In life, many have not always chosen the ideal situation, but instead the complete opposite. Even in instances, you feel you've grown tired of reliving your own version of Groundhog Day. The same patterns are completed over and over without a second thought. You relive the same emotions and put yourself through the same stress until one day you decide to do things a lot differently. Decide to do things in a way that eliminates the possibility of you having to repeat the same cycle that you have been playing out year after year. This cycle has been reintroducing you to the same disappointments. It is not beneficial and never has been.

One must become bolder, more outspoken, and true to yourself. Those around you know that you are exploding with possibility. Some may have failed to realize that your greatness is imprisoned. Autumn experienced this in various areas of her life. In the eyes of everyone that reported to her or sought advice from her; felt she had it all. What they didn't know was that she silently suffered from anxiety and seasonal affect-disorder. They had no idea how much pain rested comfortably behind her laughter and smile.

After a while, she would stop attempting to prove her worth to others and began building herself in silence. Her motivation to leap occurred after she realized how important she was along with the purpose GOD had for her. She stopped worrying about how well she played each role to everyone else. She began being faithful to the woman she was to herself. There were times when Autumn looked for the approval and confirmation of others. Suddenly, she realized that her ideas were perfect. Her style was worth it. Her time was precious. All that she stood for was great. Autumn finally came to believe that there was no need for the approval of others for her to succeed.

"Ain't no fun when the rabbit got the gun"

Once Autumn stopped giving the wrong people, unnecessary things, and bad situations, her energy; she found her joy. Her peace of mind and understanding increased. The direction she wanted to head in become extremely clear; everything that was once cloudy had a new light shone on it. When she released everything, she began to see an increase. Although many people that once had her bound ended up upset; she began to feel again. She became hopeful. She began to feel a sense of control. It was at that point in which she finally knew what it felt like to assume an enriched understanding of true empowerment. To be able to spend a day alone and not feel guilty about it was beautiful. She learned that whatever you spend the most time thinking of impacts you in every area of your life. Understand your mental/ emotional state can lead to health issues or pure bliss. Mental stability increases your ability to be more organized, structured, and make better impactful decisions. She finally realized that she wanted to be free no matter what her situation was. That said, no one can make YOU think or feel anything. Your opinion that you formulate is yours. You have a natural tenacity and charisma that will elevate you to exceptional levels. I still believe you are capable, and so should you.

Zechariah 4:6 *"Not by might nor by power, but by your spirit says the Lord of hosts."*

Spiritual Health

*Believe me when I tell you that **GOD WILL HUMBLE YOU...***

Hair laid, bills paid, and not giving one care to those throwing shade. Sometimes she wants to "flex a little bit." She sometimes wanted to flaunt what belongs to her. Autumn does not play with GOD, and you shouldn't either. Here's why. Try neglecting your relationship with GOD just because you are spending more time on or with the things that he's blessed you with. When you think that your life is perfect, and you begin passing judgment on other people; GOD will eventually show you who is BOSS. When you feel that you've got it made and believe that you can speak poorly of or about someone; GOD will show you who is more significant. When you thought that you could start giving out relationship advice and judging others; he will show you your personal and relationship flaws. Never feel that you have it all together and that you have made it to a point in life where you are untouchable. You cannot partner with GOD to have his assistance in building and sustaining you and then leave him after he elevates you. You must stay loyal to GOD's purpose and process for and in your life.

Social Health and Well-being
Never play the waiting game. You may end up wasting the best years of your life on someone or something that will not be in your future. When you know for a fact that something does not make sense; decide to move on or away because it will not benefit you to stay. Keep your mind in control of all things. Be careful not to make emotional decisions. Always look at yourself as the prize and never anything less. Listen to the facts and never the fiction that you have created in your mind.

Understand the role that you play. Try not to always blame pain, trouble, or hardship on your circumstance. Listen to what is said the first time and not the correction. Always make sure that whatever decision you make is one that will still benefit your future. Remember that people change when they are ready. This change includes you. Stop sitting around, waiting for a chance to come if you are not making the demands of yourself and those around you. If it's not about asset, benefit, growth, or progress; what are you waiting on. Do not waste your best you on procrastination. Know YOUR WORTH! Steer clear of the mental, physical, and emotional experiences that will block the blessings that GOD has in store for you.

Family Health and Wellbeing
With family; sacrifices of many types are necessary. Family relationships, at times, need massaging and truth. Everything may not always be fine, but you can't overlook the blood bond. Such a delicate relationship as the one with family allows for much pain,

betrayal, friendship, competition, and fights. Fights occur in different forms within the family circle. There is a fight to control. The battle to be heard. The struggle to be loved. The fight to be accepted. The fight to be recognized. The fight to stay connected. The fight to avoid being neglected. With so many fights of different types, there are also upsetting incidents and overheard conversations. No matter what; you are family, and ultimately, it tends to come first to all and second to none. At what point does enough become enough in overlooking things that are causing and costing you some of your most exceptional opportunities and assets in life? Who knows you best and what is truly best for you? Is it you, your family, your lover, your friend, your employer, or your finances?

Financial Health

As an aspiring business owner, your main job is to find a deal. You must find ways to profit. Real Estate has made the most millionaires in the world. Make money off your money so that you will always have money. You can either pass or fail yourself financially by making the right financial decision, having specialized knowledge, taking calculated risks, and educating yourself. Stop being afraid. Be a better, more focused asset to yourself by educating yourself in personal and business finance. You are smart enough to achieve your goals and make your dreams a reality. Give yourself more credit and feel free to step out on faith. Teach yourself how to get started through motivation, focus, and determination. Always be on the hunt for the next lead. The lead can be in saving, education, finance, and networks.

Physical Health

As a person, you must have full awareness of what your body is telling you. Your body whispers to you when it initially senses trouble. As the danger rises, your internal alarms go off sporadically to inform you of adverse impacts. Many times, we allow life and all its responsibility to silence the alarms while allowing the body to internally suffer alone until it finally runs out of back up plans and generators. We put our bodies through so much stress, tests, torments, trials, and tragedies without addressing things before emergency shutdowns occur. Time and time again, your body sends out alerts. The body tells you when it has run some systems tests, and when it is experiencing failures. We take such good care of our homes, cars, clothing, shoes, but we forget about the most important thing or being. Understand that the body is your temple, empire, and sanctuary. We owe our bodies the same priority we owe GOD who has blessed us with them. We must be careful not to poison our bodies with harmful, bagged, canned, acidic, or over-processed foods that end up causing great harm to us over time.

For years Autumn thought it was an awful thought to hear that someone was a vegan, pescatarian, or vegetarian. Her body began naturally rejecting over-processed foods and meats. As she began to complete more research, she found that there were healthier, more natural alternatives. She realized that her best days were also those that allowed for a workout. She was less stressed, and her capacity to think, be more productive and more creative came when she was eating well, exercising, and educating herself. Aside from building your external empire, you must first ensure that you have done your due diligence to take care of your body. Treat your body well, and it will reciprocate. What you do to your physical body today can either positively or negatively impact your future. Take the limits off your future by maintaining a healthy diet, regular medical check-up, and avoiding pollutants such as smoking and excessive drinking.

Professional Health

Day in and day out everyone is on their mission. They are either trying to prove themselves to themselves, an employer, a lover, a group, their families, or to their bill collectors. Some folks believe that money is the root of all evil. Others believe that money is the solution to all their problems. Some believe that upon high school graduation, one should go to college. Others have been to college and feel that they were shorted, slighted, and robbed, which in turn forced them into an unnecessary setback. The key to professional health is identification, focus, and consistency. After you have made the identification, you need to focus on learning everything there is to know about that area. Get the experience and find out about all the variations available in which you can come up with the better and the most efficient solution. Lastly, you want to consistently tap into the industry through marketing, positioning, promotion, interaction, process, production, and engagement.

Refocused- Autumn now has her energy back. A whole new burning desire to build her very own empire. Suddenly she realized that there was no longer a need for social media. Instead, she wanted out. Out of contact with anyone that could not be real with themselves, let alone someone else. She wanted away from people that zapped her of her energy. She wanted into her own. She wanted into a new beginning. With nine days into the new year; She suddenly saw that she was capable of so much more. She began to care and focus more on mind, body, and business. She craved for success in every area of her life.

She also realized that with success came separation. She could not continue to operate amongst people that were not in positive elevated mindsets. She lost interest quickly in situations where the energy levels seem to hit all-time lows. She was asked on many occasions by coworkers, direct reports, and associates; how does she keep herself motivated and spirits high in tough situations. She realized that what kept her grounded was prayer, self-determination, and her family's future positioning. She had to elevate. Everything that she was working so hard for had to work. It was not just about paying bills; it was about the future state of joy and peace. She was very much in touch with her "why."

She could not stand for her plans to blow up in her face. Every day she saw herself in a happy, loving family, with a caring, trusting, satisfied husband, beautiful, intelligent children, and an exquisite yet peace-filled home. As a professional, she saw her empire. The restaurants, apartment complexes, resorts, hotels, spas, transition homes, and multipurpose facilities. She realized that the only limit on her life was the one that she placed on herself. She realized that the life that she envisioned for herself would not be attainable with a limited mindset. Her only choice was to keep pushing through all the adversities that life planted in her path.

To be successful, you must see it, hear it, smell it, experience it, and continue to go after whatever it is that you want. Always focus on achieving goals higher than the bar that you have initially set for yourself. That means if you want a Bed and Breakfast, then you need to aim for owning a resort. If you're going to earn 10 million dollars per year, then your focus needs to be on making 100 million per year. If you always aim high, then you will never have to worry about disappointing yourself or your competition, putting you out of business.

Like Autumn, too many of us have wasted too much time on fear and folks that are afraid to move forward. The universe tells you when you are ready. You do not get to make that decision. Be prepared to receive that invitation to walk through the door of purpose and abundance. Although it may hurt to believe there will be people that you love or are in love with that you MUST leave behind. For if you don't, you could face an enormous amount of dissonance and hindrance. You will find yourself extremely frustrated having the same conversation with yourself over and over. Your internal accountability partner is gnawing at your insides. It's sending off all kinds of stress alarms. You're being urged to extinguish that fire before it burns everything down that you have worked so hard to accomplish.

Chapter 6: Natural Order

Proverbs 3:5-6
"Trust in the Lord with all your heart and lean not on your own understanding;
in all your ways submit to him, and he will make your paths straight."

Body overcome by fatigue, constant anxiety, flight of thoughts; Autumn's brain is flooded with ideas of elevation. Concerns of not living up to her fullest potential, concerned that she is not managing her money well enough, fear of doing something beautiful for herself was a constant during her quest to free herself of this on and off-again relationship with finances. Multiple jobs, associated stress, thoughts of quitting, and uncertainty all play a constant role in her fight for financial freedom. She would even guilt herself when she spent time sleeping or surfing social media for inspiration, ideas, with a hint of laughter. Autumn mentally abused herself when she found her bank account on or close to empty all because she felt that she had made too much money not to have any spare liquid assets. There were days and nights when she wishes that she was married to or dating a super-rich, loving, and supportive man. She wanted someone who could come across cash fast so that she could put some of her projects that she long to finish behind her.

She used social media to inspire herself. Many times, the only thing that scrolling social media did was make her feel like she had not accomplished enough. She did her best not to envy the rest who appeared to be more blessed — continually battling with the fact that she made a personal pact to keep her finances intact and to always have her own back. She longed for her breakthrough. So many times, she asked herself why? Why is it that everything that I have ever gotten seemed so hard to acquire? In the past, she desired a relationship with her father. Only for her to find out that before she graduated from college, his time on this earth would expire. She prayed most of her life that her mothers' indulgence in drugs would expire, but the minute she was granted her wish and more than 11 years clean; cancer would kill the woman that she looked up to as her super shero and queen.

One serious relationship after another. Only would Autumn then discover that the men she called her lover would eventually put someone or something else above her. Being regarded as someone's queen, she learned that she had many years before she would gain enough self-esteem. Finally, she discovered that it was time to put an end to putting her men above her and explore every possibility of owning her own business that her creativity and talents would uncover.

For years she wanted to write her book and even design its cover. It was not until she gotten fed up with folks who felt they were in better positions. The grand sense of entitlement, having folks say and do whatever they wanted to her; she finally felt the need to focus on things that reigned true to her. Although the quest of becoming an author was very much new to her; drive, determination, and resilience was always the glue to every broken piece that would ultimately illuminate her.

In all that you do; do not victimize yourself. Be accountable for your actions. Accept the joy that you have experienced for what it is. By no means should you leave the story unbalanced. For what is life without adrenaline and adventure. How could we truly understand joy without hurt or pain? In the same fashion, how would you know the difference between love and hate if you have never had any exposure to either? Relationships regardless of whether they are intimate, professional, or social; they all tend to invoke reminders of your past.

You never have to beg for your blessings. Instead, they fall in your lap, the phone calls come directly to you, and the requests for your services pour in. There will be no need to chase your blessings down. Naturally, all will come together without a question, doubt, or deterrence. There are so many times that one will try to be someone they are not just to live up to the expectations of the person they desire. There are instances where people play a role at work by code-switching (change of voice/ appearance to appear more socially acceptable), personality, and overall character to live up to the expectations of coworkers, colleagues, and associates. Over time this false person that you have introduced to your professional and private life grows tired, and the real you will be unveiled. It is for those reasons that I encourage you to be your true and authentic self. For what is meant will be. Forcing situations, things, and people tend to leave you empty-handed, regretful, confused, or broken. Patience allows for virtue, prosperity, joy, peace, and completion. Patience also helps you to save in many ways. As someone who wants to feed their future; you need to find contentment in where you are knowing that you will be elevated soon.

Realize that there is a sparkle within you that will help you rise to the heights in which you aim. Know that you truly are amazing just as you are. At some point in your life, you need to determine who you are and how to make who you are work for you. Understand your financial goals and the lifestyle that you want for yourself. Once you figure that out; make who you are; earn money for you. Become an influence to the people that you want to be your clients or customers. Once you begin to influence your audience, you will then be able to capitalize off of you.

You become the brand, the dream, and the reality all wrapped up in one. Just think about it. Think about how unique you are. Why conform to who the others are when you can be the brand all because no one has what you have. Guess what? At that point, you will attract others who want what you have to offer. Just like that; you have built an empire of your dreams by living and being yourself. Always understand that life happens in the exact order that it's supposed to happen. Your focus should always be on growth. As you find out exactly who you are, what you desire, and what the specifics of what you want your future to be; remember to focus on progressive actions.

Way to often do we forget that natural order rules. You can do what you want to try and force things in a different direction. The reality is; there is only but so far you will be able to make the pendulum swing with added force. Gravity will always bring it back to its rightful place. What is meant to be will be. The character an individual has will be until that individual desires to change it.

Regardless of whether fear or opportunity is a factor; you cannot force what is not meant. You may achieve your goal but understand that all things forced eventually comes crumbling down over time. Life has a strange way of showing us the power of natural order. Take a moment to think of a few marriages in which one or both parties were forced to be together. Did it withstand the test of time? Think of business ventures that were rushed; did the business withstand the test of time? Think of a meal that requires time, effort, and attention, but was prepared in a hurry. Did it pass the taste test?

Stop settling. Stop rushing. Stop worrying. Stop comparing. Stop repeating the same actions. Start preparing. Start self-evaluating. Start moving. Start focusing on you more. Start praying more. Start eating right. Start repairing your broken pieces. You are not wrecked or written off as irreparable. Start working on developing more positive energy for you. Once you are in touch with that energy, all things positive will come to you naturally. No hurt, no misunderstandings, no force, no losses, and no settling. At some point, you must be ready and willing to make some tough decisions.

We, as individuals typically endure seven stages of grief when we experience a loss of any kind. Whether the loss is of a loved one, professional, or personal; it is just that- a loss. As previously stated earlier on; you must be willing to walk away and endure the consequences of such a decision. Autumn realized that she needed to start living her life, being herself, and dismissing everyone else's thoughts, concerns, and opinions as long as she was happy, at peace, and making plenty of progress in every area of her life.

Ascension

Seven Stages of Grief

Shock & Disbelief

Life happens. Sometimes it can feel like all is suddenly beginning to fall in line. There are other times when it seems that the universe is no longer aligned in your favor. Feelings are similar to being blindsided or unexpectedly being hit by a fast-moving train when someone, a career, finances, faith, and hope is suddenly snatched away from you. It's as if you blink your eyes and everything that was- is no longer. Some stand frozen, others crumble, and there are those that immediately go into survival mode. Which are you?

There are times when losses occur in which we reason with ourselves. We many times, try to make sense of what happened. In the denial phase; you are not willing to embrace reality. Your mind can play so many tricks on you. Instead, you continue moving about completing your daily routine as if no real change has recently disrupted your norm. In this stage, you fail to accept that what is happening could be perpetuating an even harsher demise for you. Some losses are sudden while others are brought on by things we do to aid or accelerate the process. During the stage of denial, many questions are asked, and so many go unanswered. Many instances of loss allow room for excuses. There are even times when the loss is heightened to extreme devastation, given it has taken some too long to accept reality. If you, a friend, family member, or lover is stuck in this place; seek help. You must help yourself before it's too late.

Guilt

In this phase, individuals, groups, and even families tend to revisit the events that led up to the loss. Instances of self-blame can lead to self-destruction. In cases of love loss, the person that was left heartbroken tends to be left asking themselves what did I do to deserve or cause this? With job loss, many are left with the question what do I do now? How do I afford my lifestyle? Those that are confronted with the sudden death of a loved one tend to feel that they should have done more. They tend to emotionally tear themselves down with the "only if I.." statements. Ultimately the guilt stage leaves most people searching for answers or questioning their own decisions. To that, I say; do not allow a day to pass where you leave yourself plagued with questions. Try to do all that you can to fulfill each area of your life and emotional tank sufficiently.

Anger & Bargaining

When blindsided by any unpleasant events, you are at times met with mixed emotions. In instances of loss after you've overcome the initial shock, passed the denial, and surpassed the guilt; you find yourself either blaming yourself, growing resentment towards others, and possibly lashing out or wanting to release that anger in one way or another. On the other hand, you try to reason with yourself and your emotions. You have so many decisions to make internally to help create the best narrative for you. The last thing that you need to do is allow yourself to get caught up in a place of stagnation, which can very well be the place of anger. As part of the anger stage, we tend to bargain mentally and emotionally about what occurred and what could have been done differently. We allow our emotions to become a game of ping pong in our minds. This endless game prevents us from sleeping, properly functioning, and moving forward healthily. It is for those reasons that I once again remind you not to stay here too long. For you have three more stages to get to and through. Do all that you can to channel your emotions and energies. Turn your tragedy into triumph. Life could be so simple, but retaliation, anger, and insecurities make it hard.

Depression, Loneliness, & Reflection

The physical, mental, and emotional struggles we have when dealing with loss tends to fatigue us, suppress our creativity, hurt our relationship, and create ongoing traumas. Depression looks different for everyone. The one impact that it has for everyone is that it hinders progress. Counseling, support groups, and networks help to get and keep you grounded and helps lessen the impact of loneliness. As you reflect on past interactions it's good to pray, recite daily affirmations, complete journaling, and focus on goal setting as these measures although they are not a quick fix for your loss; will help to progress you.

Reconstruction & Working Through

As you get closer to acceptance, you will find that during your reconstruction, your mind will only do what you allow. If you allow yourself to be consumed with negative thoughts, feelings, and memories, then that is what you will ultimately attract into your life. During this phase, do your best to focus on moving your life, business, and emotions forward. It is imperative during this phase that you position yourself around positive people that are forward-thinking and moving. As you work through the things that you thought were going to break you; it's imperative that your focus is on the most beautiful and positive place within you. As part of this process you will need to maintain your appearance; not for others, but for the sake of where you are, where you want to be, who you are, and who you aspire to be.

Acceptance:

At this point; it is possible that you can accept; what was, what is, and what needs to be done for what is soon to come. You have embraced every aspect of what you felt was a loss for you. In this stage, you have now come to a more stable and focused place emotionally. You have found peace in what was and what is. You understand that your thoughts are whatever you choose to hold. They can now be as ugly or as beautiful as you allow. You have now regained full and total control of what you want next.

Wellness Check

Are you still holding onto past hurt, pain, regret, or sorrow?

1. _____

What do you want out of life and future relationships (business, personal, love, or social)?

2. _____

In what areas of your life can you make changes that will preserve your energy while still making progress and fulfilling your purpose?

3. _____

Are you surrounding yourself with healthy positive people?

4. _____

Are you practicing self-care?

5. _____

Have you adopted some new healthy habits?

6. _____

Have you figured out what your triggers are along with some good coping skills?

7. _____

Chapter 7: Strength in Me

Philippians 4:13 "I can do all things through Christ who strengthens me."

Teary-eyed wearing a smile she sat there and listened to them speak about the enjoyment of being able to simply up and go. Living the Y.O.L.O (You only live once) lifestyle. Traveling back and forth; always building, giving advice to others using her ideas, and getting paid from them. She simply sat there and smiled. She wanted to flip, but she thanked them instead. From the time she had her first job out of college, she prayed this prayer *"GOD help me to be content where I am knowing that you will not leave me here forever* (Stormie Omartian)."

 Each time she was pushed out of a job; due to restructuring, downsizing, position elimination, and defamation of character; she wondered how someone so dedicated as she - always ended up left out. She grew tired of this feeling in all relationships, whether it would be personal or professional. She was over the envy from those that did not know her story. She grew tired of people-pleasing. She had no time for her health and financial well- being to be at risked and continuously ending up on the chopping block. She always wondered how in every role she ended up training herself out of positions. Being blindsided and backstabbed by coworkers; Autumn would pour so much knowledge into other people. She could not understand how she became the scapegoat for those that struggled with their insecurities and being the emotional punching bag of those who would lose while she appeared to be winning.

Overwhelmed with thoughts of how to continuously survive these intense emotional beatings, she continued to press her way. Working multiple jobs to fund her business initiatives, trying to dodge all the spiteful odds stacked against her; she pushed through. She managed to accomplish many things. She was frustrated at the fact that there were so many obstacles in her path. Each obstacle seemed to cause many financial setbacks. Over time she learned that she had to focus on herself first. After leveling up; it would be time to complete the ultimate give back.

She finally realized that she needed to stop being upset with those stealing her ideas and start taking the initiative to execute them herself. She became a happier woman. Autumn had to realize that everyone around her saw the value in her ideas, but she needed to become just as hungry as everyone else who took action. She volunteered a lot of valuable insights to many people and would be upset when they made business moves that elevated them to higher ground. Autumn learned that they did what she was too lazy and afraid to do. She spoke about it, and they made moves that resulted in financial freedom and progress. She realized that she had to stop making herself out to be the victim. The reality is; no one sides with the victim when folks are already in position. Instead, you must put yourself in a position for people to recognize your body of work when they see it. The person using your work will have no choice, but to pay respects where it is due.

Being an employee often feels like you are forced into a room, the door slammed, and locked behind you, with a greedy superior yelling; WORK! They want you there in sickness and in health. Sometimes you feel as though if the laws were not present, you probably would not be able to come out or eat until the workday ends. The other dreadful part is the extreme ambivalence present when they have used you for all you are worth. There was once a time where you could feel irreplaceable at work. With cross-training and favoritism, that reality or thought process has quickly become extinct.

Alliances are formed to push out those that are not a part of the in-crowd away. They are formed due to jealousy and envy, especially when you are considered the desired, inspired, and forbidden fruit. The vultures gather, attempting to assault and assassinate your character when they smell talent and elevation headed your way. They work diligently to develop conspiracies rather than focusing on the tasks and efforts that paid them. They make the crabs stuck in the barrel look like iguanas in a pond. They act fast to cripple you but have zero motivation to do great or achieve greatness for themselves. Alone they fear confrontation, but together they present their deceptive case. Singlehanded they could not prosper, but together they create the biggest scandals. All to feed their desires and urges of the rumor mill, the water cooler conversations, the chatter that they hoped could shatter your future. Amazingly, attempts to destroy Autumn's future helped catapult her into a new career path that paid three times her original salary.

With the strength in her; she managed to be the hardest working; unemployed person one could meet after the scandal that could have shattered her emotionally. Fortunately, it only temporarily disrupted her path to success. A scandal based on lies told by one of the most significant mules in the prison system. Disruption in drug traffic caused by countless memo submissions; the mules ganged up to investigate her flaws. Unfortunately, they found one black eye that would help solidify there take. That was a boyfriend that no one could ever picture her accepting. Still, that solidified nothing.

It was not the mules that removed her; it was her honesty, desire to move on, and the fearlessness that lay deep within. She wanted an out. She was tired of her helpless profession. She helped many, but felt she was capable of so much more. She grew complacent. She also knew that if this road did not come to a screeching halt now; she would end up a future bitter bitch that *had her time.* So many of the older women there were wishing that they could have the attention of the new and old dried up male staff. It was such a tragedy to see so many desperate women working behind prison walls for decades trying to keep up with the young and tender females that came behind them — generations of bitterness. Husbands were sleeping with their wives' coworkers. Children, and grandchildren of staff were behind the bars that they held keys to.

Watching mothers come to work every day and steal commissary for their sons and grandsons from inmates whose families struggled to make a way was sickening. She was over it. Autumns career path changed, but cronyism, nepotism, and jealousy still exist. More bitter bitches stuck in the same dead-end jobs; setting those that they saw as their competition up, backstabbing, smiling faces, and constantly clout chasing. It was sickening. She knew that she was and had something special. For if she were not exceptional and not seen as a threat, she would continuously be overlooked; instead, she had the rest of the field shook.

She once heard a preacher say; be the praying woman that when you rise in the morning and your feet hit the floor; the devil yells- **Run**! She is awake. Her grandmother told her time and time again that the enemy will become your footstool. She continues to have excitement for that day. As she evolved, she realized that it is never a smart idea to put your life on hold for anyone, especially when your future is promising. Her testimony alone grew great acclaim.

Much like all the greats; she realized that to make an impact, she needed to make some significant changes in her life. Given she has had so much exposure at the ease of opportunity; she settled into what was available instead of going after what she could create. She realized that she wanted to make history in a great way. Her life had a purpose. She realized that everything that she set out to do always earned high accolades. What she stood to accept was the fact that she had to get out of her way. Autumn had to remember why she climbed, why Autumn decided that she wanted to ascend, why she is and deserves to take her royal position elegantly.

For years she cheered other women on as she watched them make history. With every gut-wrenching punch to her ego as she watched in confusion; time flew past her. YEAR after year, she set goals and crushed many of them. When it came to sustaining her own business and financial future, she seemed to hit wall after wall continuously. Meanwhile, she refused to give up. She heard people time and time again tell her that she would not be successful, but she continued to press forward against all the odds, challenges, and adversity stacked against her.

She has sat and spoke with many of the now well-known social media moguls. Some of which are even her friends. She has been encouraged by many and has given great ideas to others. Yet, she still was trying to find her own financially free place in America and on earth. She never for one second doubted that she had what it takes. She just was not as hungry as her counterparts. She realized that if she wanted to rid herself of the sleepless nights, anxiety, stress, and uncertainty of her future; she had to act now.

You can get much more accomplished when you start to prove yourself to yourself instead of abusing yourself for someone else. If you have someone in your life dragging their feet and always on the fence about everything; GET RID OF THEM. The most valuable commodity in life that can never be replaced or returned is TIME. Every second of time spent on stressful, stagnant, and dead situations tend to quadruple the mental, physical, financial, emotional, and social losses that you take. Let us take Autumn's case to help you understand the impact of years of dead relationships. Each of them needed to be terminated in their infancy. They distract you from your purpose and the more critical things in life.

After years of stressing over love and staying committed to other people's drama, she found herself experiencing extreme fatigue, migraines, sharp pains, as well as severe cramping, and near paralyzing sensations throughout her legs and back. She sought out doctor after doctor. They continuously informed her that her tests and examinations come back remarkable and that she was in phenomenal health.

Female nurse practitioners and male doctors suggested that she needed to consider pain management, but she advocated for herself. She refused to keep getting sent home with prescription medications only to return within a few days. She ruffled many feathers among medical professionals as she took matters into her own hands.

Autumn began self-monitoring, updating the providers, and informing them of suggested remedies to her condition. She was sent to specialist after specialist only to get her initial request finally fulfilled. It took the doctors nearly a year of expensive tests, and consultations before her care team finally accepted that it was worth pursuing Autumn's initial request. Had Autumn spent more time focusing on her health and business ventures than she did on dead-end relationships, she would have been able to get the treatment that she needed sooner.

Each of those emotional decisions ended up setting Autumn back years. She ended up struggling when she did not have to. She hurt when she did not need to. She spent entirely too much time focusing on the fantasy of being in a relationship rather than the grim realities of the devastating impact they had on her. Autumn spent more time learning about the men that she was dating than she did about the woman she was becoming. It was only after multiple failed attempts that she began to pay better attention to who she was, whom she wanted to become, and what her body had been telling her.

She always looked for others to tell her about her. She wanted them to help her get a handle on who she was and where she could right her wrongs. She lost herself so long ago trying to be and live up to the ideal woman that each of the men she dated wanted. The reality was that she could never be any of their ideal women because that was not who she was. She could only be herself. She sacrificed her purpose, trying to be someone she was not. She derailed many opportunities trying to be there for broken men who could never be the man she was destined to meet and marry. She sabotaged her timeline and her purpose path.

Had she spent more time on herself, she would have already become the confident woman that she became 20 years later much sooner. She wondered why she suffered from so much anxiety and lacked energy. It was because she invested it in the wrong people and places for far too long. She has been to many different empowerment engagements. While in attendance, she knew that one of the notorious questions that would come up for each group was "what's your WHY?" Currently; she knows hers, but what's YOURS?

Thank you...

Thank you for taking time out of your busy schedule to grow with me. It is my hope and prayer that you were able to grow through what you have recently read through. It is my desire for you to have completed some much-needed self-reflection and inventory. I hope that as you read this book, you were able to pat yourself on the back for avoiding some of the blunders that were mentioned. I hope that if you have found yourself confronted with any of the scenarios presented; that you now feel equipped to effectively combat some of the obstacles that you have once faced.

Thank you for also being willing enough to step out on faith and begin working on every area of your life. In so many instances, we try to financially stabilize while forgetting how much of a mess is present in the other six areas of our lives. Instead, you finally grew to accept that it is time to tackle the whole person that is YOU. Thank you for having a desire to present a healthier self-aware version of who you are and taking additional steps towards offering an even more robust version of who you want to be.

At this time, I would like to present to you the thought process behind the colors as I initially promised at the beginning of the book.

__Significance of Colors__

I have chosen to make the base color for this book turquoise. The color turquoise signifies good health, clarity, calm, emotional balance, sophistication, positivity, wisdom, spiritual grounding, love, loyalty, friendship, intuition, open communication, good luck, serenity, joy, creativity, patience, wholeness, energy, tranquility, and is also known to be refreshing. It is for those reasons and many more I aspired to bring forth all things positive as you read *Ascension*.

Gold represents winning, wealth, success, quality, victory, extravagance, illumination, passion, courage, prestige, affluence, luxury, elegance, prosperity, value, glamour, wisdom, sophistication, status, and ultimately influences the course of events. In almost all competitions; the winner is victoriously crowned with a piece of gold of some sort. It is for so many of the previously mentioned reasons that I have decided to sprinkle some gold all over every winner and all royalty who reads this book.

In all competitions, the goal of the greatest majority is to win. On the flip side; there are those that simply want to finish. That said, I would not refer to such individuals as competitors, but instead participants. Given their participation is solely based on completion; this translates as a win for self without having a goal to hold a position in power, claim a title, or be recognized by others as the best which helps to solidify my stance. With that being said, I will assume that you have read this book as someone who wants to win and claim your position; not only publicly, but internally. Understanding the audience that this piece would appeal to; gold was incorporated into the cover.

White is typically associated with purity, goodness, and freshness. One who ascends generally has found a new start, elevation, and beginning of something better. Soon you will begin to shed the negativity, open the box of emotions that lay dormant in your mind, and release. As you take this beautiful journey of evolution; I hope that you will feel a sense of freedom, relief, and a new emotional start.

The butterfly was chosen because it symbolizes the finding of joy in life. As you may already know; there are so many variations of adversity encountered by a caterpillar. Secondly, there is isolation and incubation as it matures while in the cocoon. Thirdly, there is the fight to break free from the cocoon. Lastly, there is the emergence of the butterfly from the cocoon, which unveils the final beauty and reward after the evolution into the most beautiful art form of GOD's creation. The reward for the caterpillar turned butterfly is the earned wings signifying freedom, peace, and elevation after overcoming every obstacle faced during the transition. This transition is the very same way you too will evolve as a seasoned professional and business owner. You too will potentially reflect on your tragedies and triumphs in juxtaposition to the butterfly as you experience your own Ascension.

Go get everything that you deserve and more. You are unstoppable. You deserve a better lifestyle, life partner, and financial positioning. It's time. PUSH THROUGH… GOD Bless…

ABOUT THE AUTHOR

Philadelphia native, Ebonye S. White, grew up in the inner city where she attended Simon Gratz Highschool. She shares her professional knowledge and skills with young people throughout her hometown. She lost both of her parents prior to graduating college.

Ebonye earned her bachelor's degree from Hampton University. She later went on to earn her master's degree from the University of Pennsylvania. She has always strived to be and do her best as well as surround herself with the best. Over the years she has embraced and referred to herself as a *woman on the grow*. She believes that for one to ascend you must always be willing to learn and grow.

With a life plagued with emotionally crippling challenges; she managed to start a lucrative career in the medical technology field. She eventually fell in love with real estate and become rather successful in an area she loves. Ebonye prides herself in progressing against all odds and adversities stacked against her while motivating others in the process.

Made in the USA
Lexington, KY
02 December 2019